Betty
goes bananas
in her Pyjamas

Steve Antony

The moon was out. The stars were shining.
And Betty was playing in her bedroom.

'It is time for you
to go to bed,'
said Mr Toucan.

But suddenly . . .

BANANAS

Instead, Betty wanted to . . .

and her xylophone,

TING!
TING!

and her trumpet,

BARP!

until finally . . .

'Maybe you should go to
your soft, warm bed.'

'After a good night's sleep,
you can play more music tomorrow.'

But suddenly . . .

'I don't want to go to bed.'

Instead,
Betty wanted to . . .

paint a flower,

SPLISH!

and a dinosaur,

SPLASH!

and a butterfly,

SPLAT!

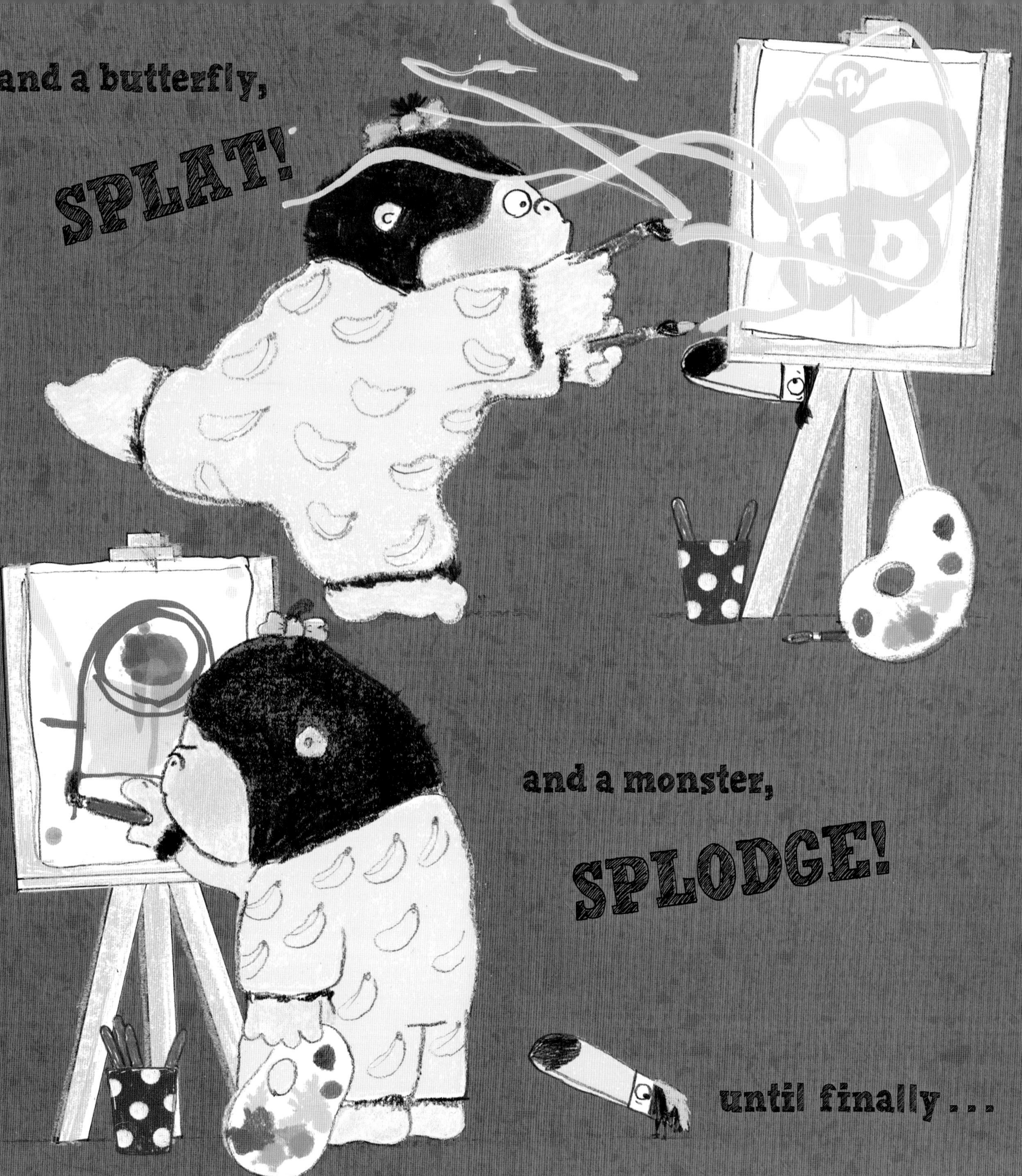

and a monster,

SPLODGE!

until finally . . .

'Maybe you should go to bed with your big, cuddly teddy bear.'

'After a good night's sleep, you can paint more pictures tomorrow.'

But Betty . . .

played with her car,

BEEP! BEEP!

and her lorry,

HONK! HONK!

'You can play with ALL
of your toys tomorrow.'

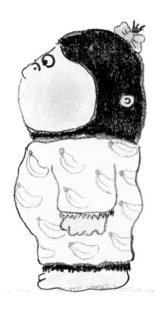

'If you go to bed right now . . .

'I will read you a
BEDTIME STORY.'

Betty enjoyed her bedtime story so much that she wanted to hear it . . .

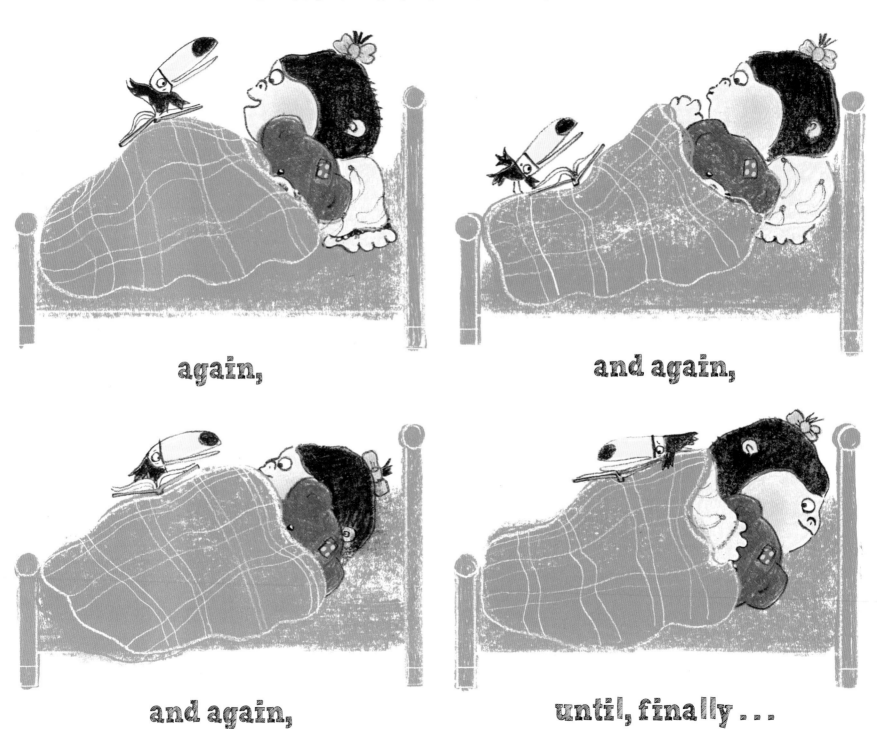

again,

and again,

and again,

until, finally . . .

she was fast asleep.

The moon was out. The stars were shining.
And all was quiet in Betty's bedroom.

'Goodnight, Betty,'
said Mr Toucan.

Z

Then suddenly . . .

CRASH!

To Mum, the best storyteller ever,
and all other Toucans.

OXFORD
UNIVERSITY PRESS

Great Clarendon Street, Oxford, OX2 6DP,
United Kingdom

Oxford University Press is a department of the University of Oxford.
It furthers the University's objective of excellence in research,
scholarship, and education by publishing worldwide. Oxford is a
registered trade mark of Oxford University Press in the UK and in
certain other countries

Text and illustrations © Steve Antony 2015
The moral rights of the author have been asserted

Database right Oxford University Press (maker)

First Edition published in 2015

British Library Cataloguing in Publication Data available

ISBN: 978-0-19-273818-9 (hardback)
ISBN: 978-0-19-273819-6 (paperback)
ISBN: 978-0-19-273820-2 (eBook)

1 3 5 7 9 10 8 6 4 2

Printed in China

Paper used in the production of this book is a natural, recyclable
product made from wood grown in sustainable forests.
The manufacturing process conforms to the environmental
regulations of the county of origin.